I0530926

Love's Anchor

A Steamy, Small-Town Friends-to-Lovers Romance Between a Stubborn Bar Owner and a No-Nonsense Cop

Hana York

Pink Pop Publishing

Love's Anchor

(Hearts on Duty Book 2)

Copyright © 2025 by Hana York

All rights reserved.

www.HanaYork.com

Contents

Chapter One

♥

THEO

Sunlight streamed through the shattered windows of the Rusty Anchor, throwing long shadows over the wreckage—broken glass, toppled barstools, and the gut-wrenching sight of my once-pristine bar reduced to chaos. My bar. My sanctuary. And some bastard had come in here and wrecked it like it meant nothing. My jaw tightened, fists clenching at my sides. Whoever did this? They were going to pay.

The bell above the door jingled, and my muscles tensed. A sound that usually meant regulars stopping by for a drink now sent a prickle of unease down my spine. I turned to see Brooke Taylor step inside, her badge catching the morning light.

Brooke and I had been friends for years, the kind of friendship built on late-night conversations shared beers, and the unspoken understanding that she always had my back, on and off duty. And I always had hers. She was steady, no-nonsense, and knew me better than most. Lately, though, something had shifted. Maybe it was just me; maybe it was nothing. But standing there, anger still simmering in my chest, my gaze caught on the determined set of her jaw, the sharp focus in her eyes, and for the first time, I wondered—if I reached for her, would she pull away or lean in?

"Morning," she said, her voice calm, cutting through my jumbled thoughts. Her sharp gaze flickered over the destruction, cataloging every detail for the second time. "I couldn't stop thinking about this place last night. Thought I'd stop by and see how you're holding up."

A ghost of a smile tugged at my lips. "Aw, worried about me? I'm touched."

Brooke shot me a flat look. "The bar, Morgan. I'm asking about the bar."

"Ah," I said, letting out a dry laugh. "Total disaster zone. Though I'm considering rebranding—thinking 'artfully distressed' has a nice ring to it."

Brooke arched a brow. "I think 'trashed' is the word you're looking for."

"Nice to see you haven't lost your charm, Officer Taylor," I drawled, crossing my arms.

She took a step closer, flipping open her notepad. "Alright, let's go through this again. Anything new come to mind?"

I exhaled sharply, shaking my head. "Dead end. If I had even a hint of something useful, you'd be slapping cuffs on someone instead of us standing here looking like idiots."

Brooke let out a weary sigh. She crouched by the broken window, carefully studying its jagged edges, her ponytail swaying with each slight movement.

She straightened, leveling me with that no-nonsense stare of hers. "Are you going to help me figure this out, or are you planning to stand there brooding all day?"

I smirked. "I can brood and help. I'm nothing if not multi-talented."

For a moment, our eyes locked, and the air shifted—something unspoken crackling between us. It wasn't just the break-in messing with my head. It was her. The way she stood there, determined as ever, acting like she had everything under control when I knew damn well she cared more than she let on.

After a moment, she sank into a chair, flipping open her notepad. Her pen tapped against the wood in a steady rhythm, the only sound cutting through the eerie silence that had taken over the bar—no music, no conversations, just the aftermath of destruction. I stood behind the counter, rearranging bottles that didn't need rearranging, my fingers tightening around the glass as the restless energy inside me refused to settle.

"You're going to wear a groove into that counter," Brooke muttered without looking up.

I paused mid-motion, glancing over at her with a raised brow. "Would you rather I pace? Might add some drama to your 'crime scene'."

She smirked, finally looking up from her notes. "Did anyone stand out last week? Someone acting off, asking weird questions?"

Leaning against the bar, I tried to think back. "Not really. The usual crowd—regulars, tourists stopping in before heading to the bay. Nothing that screamed 'future vandal'."

Brooke jotted something down, her pen moving fast. "What about your staff? Anyone mention seeing someone hanging around after closing?"

I shook my head. "If they did, they didn't tell me. But I'll ask. They're supposed to come by later to help clean up."

"Good," she said, snapping her notebook shut. "I'll need to talk to them too."

I studied her, taking in the tightness of her jaw, the way her fingers tapped against her notepad—a little too forcefully, a little too restless. This wasn't just another case for her.

"You're taking this personally." My voice was steady, watching for the tell in her reaction.

Her gaze flicked up, guarded. "It's my job."

I leaned in slightly, lowering my voice. "It's more than that, and we both know it. You were here within ten minutes of my call last night, Brooke. This feels different."

Something passed through her expression—hesitation, conflict, maybe something she didn't want me to see. For a second, I thought she'd brush it off. Instead, she sighed, her shoulders losing that stubborn edge.

"I hate seeing this happen to you." Her voice was quieter now, but the weight behind it hit me harder than I expected. "To the Anchor. It's one of the few places in this town that feels... real. And I don't like seeing people mess with that or..." She trailed off, her thought unfinished.

Something pulled tight in my chest. A part of me wanted to push, to ask what she wasn't saying. But another part of me—the one that had spent years pretending she wasn't the first person I looked for in a crowded room—wasn't ready to unpack that.

So I smirked instead, tilting my head. "My knight in shining armor, huh?"

Brooke rolled her eyes, but there was a twitch at the corner of her lips—like she was fighting a smile. "Don't flatter yourself."

Still, I caught the way her gaze lingered on me for half a second too long.

"What about security tapes?" she asked, pen poised over her notepad.

I hesitated, shifting slightly, my fingers absently brushing over my sleeve. "Right. That."

Her brows lifted. "That?"

I exhaled, rubbing the back of my neck. "The whole system's been glitchy as hell lately. Cameras keep cutting in and out. I've been putting off getting it fixed."

Brooke's pen stopped mid-stroke, hovering over the notepad. She blinked once, then slowly set it down, leveling me with a look that sent a prickle of awareness down my spine. "And this didn't seem worth mentioning earlier because...?"

The weight of her stare was almost worse than if she'd just let out one of those disappointed sighs.

I dragged a hand through my hair. "Didn't think it was relevant." A pause. "...Clearly, I was wrong."

Brooke inhaled slowly, pressing her fingers against her temples like she was trying to will away the urge to strangle me. "Well, might as well check it out. Maybe we'll get lucky."

I doubted it.

But right now, we could use all the luck we could get.

BROOKE

Theo led me into his back office, a space that could generously be described as organized chaos. Papers were stacked in precarious towers on every available surface, one wrong move away from an avalanche. I crossed my arms, watching as he wrestled with the bar's outdated computer system, his fingers drumming impatiently on the ancient keyboard.

"That thing belongs in a museum," I muttered, eyeing the bulky thing like it might wheeze its last breath.

"Easy there," Theo said, gently patting the monitor. "She's a classic, not a fossil."

I rolled my eyes. "You're impossible."

"True," he said, shooting me that familiar grin. "But at least I'm entertaining."

He wasn't wrong. Even in the middle of this mess, he made things feel lighter. It was just... Theo. Steady, familiar, safe. And yet, as I leaned against the wall, something about this moment felt different.

The security footage started loading, and the screen flickered to life the grainy images processed. I stepped closer, drawn in, until my shoulder brushed against his. He tensed, just for a second, before adjusting the controls. I told myself it was nothing. Just nerves. Just stress.

But the tiny spark where we touched lingered longer than it should have.

"Look," I whispered, pointing to the screen as a shadowed figure slipped past the camera.

Theo hit pause, leaning in. His brows drew together as he studied the figure. "Can't tell who that is. Hood's up. Dark clothing. Not much to go on."

My stomach tightened as we watched the intruder wreck the place—flipping tables, smashing bottles, tearing apart what Theo had built. A muscle ticked in his jaw, his hands curling into fists.

"Can you zoom in?" I asked, tension tightening my voice.

He fiddled with the controls, but the closer we got, the worse the image became—just pixels and shadows where a face should be.

"Back it up," I said, stepping closer without thinking. "Maybe we can catch them walking in."

Theo rewound the footage, his fingers unsteady on the keyboard. The small office suddenly felt even smaller. I could smell the faint trace of his cologne—warm, woodsy, familiar. My gaze flicked to the curve of his jaw, the way his dark stubble shadowed his skin.

I swallowed hard, forcing my focus back to the screen.

"Stop!" I exclaimed, gripping his arm as movement flashed across the screen.

Theo froze the frame, his body going rigid beneath my touch.

Electricity shot up my arm. I should have let go. I didn't.

On the screen, the hooded figure slipped in through the back door, face turned away from the camera.

"Damn," Theo muttered. "Still can't see their face."

The footage played on, the intruder moving with unsettling confidence. No hesitation. No confusion.

"They knew the layout," I murmured, barely aware of how close I'd gotten to Theo. "The exact route. This was planned, Theo. Every step."

He turned to me then, eyes sharp and searching. "Yeah," he said quietly, his voice rough. "Which means it probably isn't over."

The weight of his words settled between us, thick with things left unsaid, things I wasn't ready to name. And not for the first time since this started, my thoughts drifted somewhere they shouldn't.

I wasn't just thinking about the case.

I was thinking about Theo.

About the way his presence filled the space beside me, steady and familiar—but suddenly different. About the way my pulse had started reacting to him in a way I couldn't ignore.

Maybe, just maybe, I wasn't as immune to him as I'd convinced myself I was.

Theo shifted beside me, the brush of his arm against mine barely there—but enough to send a flicker of awareness through me. But I forced my attention back to the screen, studying every flickering frame like the answers I really needed were buried somewhere in the footage.

"But why target the Rusty Anchor?" he murmured, his voice lower now, rougher.

I dragged my gaze away from the footage. Theo was watching me—but not in the way I was used to. There was no easy smirk, no teasing glint in his eyes. His expression was unreadable, his dark gaze heavy with something else.

Something dangerous.

My throat tightened.

"I don't know," I whispered, barely hearing my voice over the pounding in my ears. "We'll figure this out."

Theo exhaled slowly, his eyes still locked on mine, searching like he wasn't sure we were still discussing the case.

"We have to," I added, more for myself than for him.

Because if I let myself think about what was happening between us, whatever this was, I wasn't sure I'd be able to stop it.

And I wasn't sure I wanted to.

Chapter Two

THEO

A loud crash shattered the silence.

I jolted, instincts kicking in before my mind could process the sound. Brooke stiffened beside me, both of us turning toward the bar.

Whatever was happening between us would have to wait. Because something—or someone—had just made that crash.

"We should... we should check that out," Brooke said, her voice uneven.

I nodded, not trusting myself to speak, and followed her out of the office. My thoughts weren't where they should be. Not on the bar, not on the break-in—but on her. On the way she'd looked at me in those few breathless seconds before the interruption, like we were standing at the same edge, both of us knowing damn well that once we fell, we'd fall together.

The main room was exactly as we'd left it, except for the fresh mess along the far wall—shattered bottles, broken glass, liquor bleeding into the floorboards like an open wound.

Brooke swept her gaze over the room, all business again, like she hadn't almost kissed me in the dark of my office.

"Shelf couldn't hold its liquor," she muttered, the dry humor undercut by the slight shake of her hand as she tucked her notepad away.

I exhaled slowly, trying to push past the heat still coiled tight in my chest. "Yeah. That spot's been loose forever. Break-in finally did it in, I guess."

I should have been focused on the damage. But all I could think about was the damage she was doing to my self-control.

I crouched to gather the larger shards, but Brooke's hand closed around my arm, stopping me.

I froze.

Her grip was firm but careful, her fingers warm against my skin. I turned, expecting her to let go—but she didn't.

"Let me help," she said softly, her voice different this time. Less practical. More personal. "You shouldn't have to deal with this alone."

Something tightened in my chest.

I should've told her I was fine. That I didn't need help. That I was used to handling things on my own.

But I couldn't make myself say it.

So I just nodded.

And together, we started picking up the pieces.

My trashed bar needed my attention.

But all I could think about was kissing her.

Of finally closing the distance.

Of letting myself take what I'd been craving for too damn long.

"You know," I said, breaking the thick silence, "this isn't exactly how I pictured getting you behind the bar."

Brooke glanced up, amusement flickering in her blue eyes. "Oh? And how did you picture it?"

I leaned against the counter, letting my gaze drag over her just to see if she'd notice. "Well, for starters, there'd be a lot less broken glass... and a lot more tequila."

She rolled her eyes, but the faint flush creeping up her neck told me she wasn't immune to how I looked at her.

"In your dreams, Morgan," she said, shaking her head.

I grinned, voice dropping lower. "Oh, trust me. My dreams? They don't just stop at getting you behind the bar. More like on the bar..."

Brooke went rigid for half a second before she recovered, busying herself with wiping down the counter. I watched her, admiring how her uniform hugged her curves, the way her lips pressed together like she was willing herself not to react.

She felt it, too. I knew it.

"You're staring," she muttered, still not looking at me.

"Can you blame me?" I shot back, my voice rougher than I intended.

When she met my gaze this time, something flickered behind her eyes—something dark, something dangerous.

My pulse kicked up. How long had we been doing this? Dancing around the inevitable?

Years of history stretched between us, thick with tension we never dared acknowledge. I still remembered the first time she walked into my bar—fresh out of the academy, sharp-eyed, too damn confident for her own good. She'd looked at me like she could see straight through me.

And I'd been hooked.

But Brooke Taylor wasn't the kind of woman you risk losing. So I kept my distance. Kept things friendly. Kept it safe.

Until now.

"Theo," she whispered, barely audible over my hammering heart. "We can't..."

I stepped closer, pulled in by something I no longer wanted to fight.

"Can't what?" My voice was low, measured, as I watched her—really watched her. "Can't admit this is real? That we've both felt it for years?"

She sucked in a sharp breath, her resolve cracking like glass.

I could smell the faint traces of her shampoo—citrus and something soft beneath it, wrapped in the warmth of coffee from earlier. Her scent curled around me and dragged me under.

I reached out, letting my fingers just barely graze the inside of her wrist. She shivered.

"You know why," she murmured, but her voice lacked conviction. "I'm on duty. And this is... complicated."

I exhaled sharply, tilting my head as I studied her face. The woman who had been my best friend for years. The woman I'd wanted for just as long.

"Life's complicated, Brooke." My voice was barely above a whisper. "Doesn't mean we can't take a chance on something good."

At my words, she leaned in. Just enough for my breath to catch.

My fingers traced up her arm, slow and deliberate, following the curve of her shoulder. Goosebumps rose beneath my touch, her pulse hammering against my fingertips. Her lips parted slightly like she was waiting—like she wanted me to close the space between us.

And God help me, I was already leaning in.

The sharp crackle of her police radio shattered the moment.

Brooke jerked back like she'd been burned, scrambling for the radio at her hip.

"Officer Taylor, come in," the dispatcher's voice crackled through the static.

She swallowed hard, her voice uneven as she answered. "Taylor here. Go ahead."

"We've got a situation down at the marina. Multiple boats were reported vandalized. Chief wants all available units."

She exhaled sharply, stepping further away from me. "Copy that. I'm on my way."

Her eyes flicked to mine, an apology written all over her face. "I have to go."

I nodded, shoving my hands into my pockets to avoid reaching for her again. "Duty calls, huh?"

"Yeah," she murmured, already heading for the door. "I'll... I'll check in later, okay?"

I didn't respond. I stood there, watching her walk away, knowing damn well she wasn't just answering a call—she was running from what almost happened between us.

The second the door shut behind her, I took a long breath and ran a hand through my hair. My pulse was still hammering, the weight of what nearly happened pressing down on me.

The difference between us? She still thought she could ignore it.

I wasn't so sure I could anymore.

Chapter Three

♥

BROOKE

I dragged myself up the stairs to my apartment, every muscle in my body protesting with each step. What a damn day.

What started as vandalism at the marina had spiraled into a full-blown investigation—hours of taking statements, analyzing evidence, and dealing with boat owners who were all too eager to demand justice. By the time I finally clocked out, night had settled over Anchor Bay, and my head was swimming with too many theories and too little patience.

I paused at my front door, exhaling hard. The case should have been the only thing on my mind. But somehow, my thoughts kept circling back to Theo.

My fingers hovered over the lock as I replayed how he'd looked at me in the bar, the heat in his eyes burning through my defenses. My skin still hummed with the memory of his touch, his hand grazing my cheek, his breath warm against mine. God, I had been so close to kissing him.

I shook my head, clearing the thought away as I stepped inside. That was tomorrow's problem. Right now, I just needed a hot shower and enough sleep to stop my brain from running in circles.

Shedding my uniform, I padded barefoot to the bathroom and twisted the shower knob until steam curled through the air. The second the hot water hit my skin, I let out a deep sigh, tilting my head back, trying and failing to let the tension melt away.

But instead of finding peace, my mind drifted right back to Theo.

Damn it.

I could still feel the brush of his fingers along my arm, the unspoken tension in the space between us. How he'd said my name—low and rough—causing heat to pool between my thighs.

I bit my lip, remembering how his gaze had lingered on mine, the raw pull simmering between us for years finally bubbling over. If that call hadn't come in, if we hadn't been interrupted...

Would I have kissed him?

I wanted to. God help me, I wanted to.

But Theo wasn't just some fleeting crush I could ignore or a mistake I could shrug off in the morning. He was Theo. A constant in my life.

And that made this so much more dangerous.

I shut off the water and grabbed a towel, bracing myself as reality settled back in. I had a job to do. I couldn't afford distractions—especially ones that came with hazel eyes and a smirk that could break me.

As I walked into my bedroom, my phone chimed from the night-stand. I barely had to look at the screen to know who it was.

Theo.

"Hey, you doing alright after everything?"

A slow, familiar warmth spread through my chest. My fingers hovered over the keyboard before I typed back:

"Been better, but I'll live. How goes clean up?"

His response came almost instantly.

"Not as terrible as we thought. Got it looking halfway normal again. Want to swing by tomorrow and see?"

I hesitated, his words pressing deeper than they should. I could almost hear his voice, the casual ease masking something heavier—something we still hadn't acknowledged.

My fingers hovered over the keyboard, debating.

"I'll try to swing by."

Theo's reply came quickly.

"Looking forward to it. Sweet dreams, Officer Taylor."

Damn him.

I tossed my phone onto the nightstand and slid under the covers, my skin still tingling from the shower, my mind unwilling to let go of Theo.

The way he touched me. The way he looked at me.

The way I wanted him to do it again.

And for the first time in a long time, sleep didn't come easy.

THEO

I stared at Brooke's message, reading it repeatedly as if the words might shift and enlighten me. *"I'll try to swing by."*

She was thinking about it. Thinking about me.

I could practically picture her hunched over her phone, typing and deleting a dozen times before settling on those five words. Classic Brooke. Always cautious, always overanalyzing—except when she was on the job. Then she was sharp, instinctive, never second-guessing. But when it came to us? Yeah, she hesitated. And I got it.

I leaned back against the bar, scanning the place. The cleanup crew had done their job well enough—anyone walking in tomorrow wouldn't suspect a thing had happened. But I knew better. Something about this break-in felt personal, and I couldn't shake the feeling that it wasn't over.

Still, my mind wasn't on the bar anymore. It was on her.

I exhaled sharply, rubbing my palm over my jaw as flashes of the morning played on repeat. Brooke standing close—so damn close. Her breath hitching when I touched her cheek, and her fingers trembling momentarily before she pulled back.

For years, I'd kept my distance. Made excuses. Played it safe. But that moment? That crackling pull between us?

Maybe fate was done waiting for me to get my shit together.

I clicked off the lights, locking up before stepping into the cool night air. The breeze hit my face like a slap—a welcome distraction from the heat still simmering in my blood. I walked home slowly, trying to shake off the restlessness crawling under my skin, but my thoughts kept circling back to her.

Damn it.

Every step toward my apartment only worsened the tension, winding through my muscles like a spring ready to snap. Once home, I stripped off my shirt and the rest of my clothes, letting them fall to the floor before stepping into the shower. I cranked the water hotter than necessary, hoping to clear my head.

As steam filled the bathroom, I closed my eyes and let my mind wander. I imagined Brooke with me, her lithe body pressed against mine under the steaming water. My hand drifted down my chest as I pictured her slender fingers tracing the same path. In my mind, her sapphire eyes gazed up at me, dark with desire, as she pressed her body flush against mine. I imagined the soft curves of her breasts against my chest, her hardened nipples grazing my skin.

A low groan escaped my lips as my hand wrapped around my hardening length. I stroked slowly, picturing Brooke's delicate hand in place of my own. In my fantasy, she teased me with feather-light touches before gripping me firmly. I braced one hand against the shower wall as I increased my pace. I imagined Brooke's lips on my neck, trailing kisses down my chest. My breath came in ragged pants as I pictured her on her knees before me, her pink tongue darting out to taste me, her lips wrapping around my throbbing length. My hand moved faster as the fantasy took hold.

I pictured lifting Brooke, pinning her against the shower wall as I thrust into her tight heat. I imagined the way she'd gasp my name, her nails raking down my back as I drove into her again and again. "Fuck, Brooke," I ground out, my strokes quickening. My hips jerked as I imagined her tight heat enveloping me. I pictured her legs wrapped around my waist, urging me deeper. In my mind, I could hear her breathy moans and feel her pussy clenching around me as I brought her closer to the edge.

With a few final strokes, I came with a muffled groan, my release washing over me in waves of pleasure. I braced against the shower wall, panting as the last aftershocks rippled through my body. Reality slowly filtered back in as the water washed away the evidence of my fantasy. I turned off the shower and stepped out, wrapping a towel around my waist. I caught sight of myself in the foggy mirror—flushed cheeks, tousled hair, eyes still dark with desire.

I released an unsteady breath as guilt and desire battled inside me. I'd pictured Brooke before—countless times, but never like this. The fresh memory of her at the bar—her body close to mine, that small catch in her breath when my fingers grazed her skin—made my past fantasies feel like pale imitations of the real thing.

All I could see now was Brooke. Not as my friend. Not as the cop who always had my back. But as the woman I wanted.

I clenched my jaw and exhaled roughly, forcing myself to let it go.

She wasn't here. And until she wanted to be, I had to respect that.

But that didn't change the truth—I was done pretending.

As I crawled into bed, the lingering heat of my release wasn't enough to quiet the storm in my head. Something had changed today.

That moment in the bar—the almost-kiss, how Brooke had looked at me—cracked something open between us. Something we'd spent years ignoring, burying under sarcastic banter and unspoken truths. And now?

Now, there was no going back.

A slow grin tugged at my lips as exhaustion finally pulled me under.

Tomorrow.

Tomorrow, I'd see her. And if I had anything to say about it, we wouldn't pretend nothing had happened. Not this time.

Chapter Four

♥

BROOKE

The Rusty Anchor had hit its afternoon lull, with just the die-hard regulars left clutching their glasses. Low voices mixed with the gentle ping of bottles and tumblers, filling the quiet. At the bar's edge, I hunched over my notepad, drumming my pen against the paper while the case chipped away at my patience.

This wasn't just about Theo's bar anymore.

One break-in could be bad luck. Two? Maybe coincidence. But we were past that. Three, four, five businesses hit in just a few months? That was a pattern—one I couldn't ignore.

"You're going to wear a hole in that page."

Theo's voice cut through my thoughts, dragging me back to the present.

I looked up, irritation flickering in my chest. "This wasn't random," I said, shaking my head. "They knew exactly what they were doing."

Theo tossed his rag onto the counter, arms crossing over his chest. "You certain about that?"

I flipped through my notes, frustration bubbling up. "Look at the pattern." I spread the pages out, tapping a pen against the list of businesses. "It's obvious. Every single target has been a local mom-and-pop shop. Someone's trying to gut the neighborhood, one small business at a time."

His jaw tightened as he leaned against the bar. "What kind of person goes after places like that?"

"I'm working on finding out," I muttered, scanning the notes again. It felt like I was missing something, the final piece that would make all this click.

"Any leads?" He shifted forward in his chair.

I rubbed my temples with a heavy sigh. "Nothing solid. But my instincts say we're looking local. The timing's too calculated, too exact—whoever it is knows this town like their own backyard."

Theo ran a hand through his hair, his expression darkening. "What if we're looking at this wrong?" he mused, stepping closer. "Maybe what they took isn't the point. Maybe it's about sending a message."

I straightened, intrigued. "Go on."

He leaned in, his voice low and steady. "All these hits on local shops? Someone could be trying to drive us out. Make room for chain stores, maybe developers?"

My pulse kicked up. "Damn," I whispered, flipping through my notes. "That... that actually makes sense." A name popped out at me, one that had been buried in the reports but suddenly felt glaring. "Rick Hayes. That name mean anything to you?"

Theo's expression darkened instantly. His hands curled into fists against the bar. "Rick Hayes? That slimy son of a bitch tried to buy out my family's old bar years ago. When my parents refused to sell, suddenly, they were hit with health code violations, noise complaints, you name it. Eventually, they couldn't keep up with the fines and had to close down."

I stared at him, stunned. "Theo, why didn't you ever tell me about this?"

He shrugged, looking away. "Ancient history. Or so I thought."

"Not so ancient anymore," I muttered, furiously scribbling notes. "This could be the break we needed. If Hayes is behind these attacks..."

"Then he's graduated from shady business practices to outright criminal activity," Theo finished grimly. "Where do we start?"

I snapped my notebook shut and met his gaze. "There is no 'we' here," I said firmly. "This is my case."

Theo took a step toward me, his voice dropping low. "You can't ice me out on this one, Brooke. We both know what this means to me."

"Which is precisely why you need to stay out of it," I fired back, planting my feet. "You're in too deep."

"Don't you dare shut me out," Theo snarled.

I let out a sharp breath, willing my tone to be gentle. "I'm just trying to keep you safe," I said softly. "Let me do my job. If Rick's behind this, I'll take him down. But I can't focus if I'm worried about you jumping into the fire and getting burned."

The tension between us was thick, wrapping around the air like an unspoken challenge. Theo stared at me, clearly hating the idea of standing on the sidelines. I could see it in the set of his jaw, the way his hands clenched at his sides.

Finally, he heaved a heavy sigh. "Fine. But if you need anything—anything at all—you let me know."

Relief flickered through me, though I tried not to let it show too much. "I will," I promised.

I turned back to my notepad, jotting down a few final thoughts, but I could feel Theo's eyes on me. The weight of his stare sent a shiver down my spine.

I knew letting me take the lead didn't sit right with him. It wasn't in Theo's nature to step aside when something—or someone—he cared about was at risk.

I cleared my throat. "I need to get back to the station. Hayes' background might give us something to work with."

Theo gave a slow nod. "Yeah, makes sense."

I gathered my things quickly, but my fingers trembled slightly. I avoided his gaze, knowing if I met it, I might not leave.

"Hey," Theo said, his voice quieter now, pulling me to a stop. "Just... watch yourself out there. If Hayes is involved—"

"I'll be careful," I interrupted, finally forcing myself to look up at him. His hazel eyes were filled with concern, frustration, and something unspoken. "I promise."

Without thinking, I reached out, my fingers brushing against his arm. His breath hitched—just enough for me to notice—and for a brief moment, I let myself stay there, my palm resting lightly against the warmth of his skin.

"We're in this together," I said softly, meaning every word.

Theo didn't move, didn't even blink. The air between us shifted and thickened. His fingers twitched at his side like he debated whether to reach for me or pull me in. But he didn't. He stayed still, holding my gaze in a way that made my pulse pound.

"Together," he echoed.

I let my hand linger for a second longer than I should have before I pulled away. "I'll call you if I find anything."

I turned toward the door, forcing myself to walk away, to put space between us before I did something reckless.

THEO

As soon as Brooke slipped out the door, the bell jingling softly behind her, I let out a slow breath. My thoughts spun, a tangled mess of frustration and anger. My grip tightened on the edge of the bar, fingers pressing into the wood as I tried to steady myself.

Rick Hayes. Even the name made my blood boil. The memories came rushing back—the day my parents had to lock up their bar for good, their dream ripped out from under them by a man who saw nothing but dollar signs. Hayes had gutted their future, twisted the knife, and walked away without a second thought.

And now he was back.

I couldn't just stand by and let Brooke handle this alone. I knew she thought she was protecting me, keeping me from getting in too deep, but this was personal. Hayes had already taken one piece of my life—I wasn't about to let him take another.

I strode toward the office, flipping on the computer. The ancient thing groaned as it powered up, but I didn't have time to wait for it to catch up. My fingers tapped impatiently on the desk as I searched for anything on Hayes. Real estate transactions, business filings, development plans—anything that would tell me what he was after this time.

And then, I found it.

Bayside Ventures. A slick corporate name masking the same dirty game. Several small businesses in the area had been bought up in the last six months, all local and struggling just enough to make a buyout seem appealing. And there, buried in the fine print, was Rick Hayes—silent partner.

"Gotcha, you bastard," I muttered, leaning back in my chair.

I should've called Brooke right then. Should've given her the information and let her handle it.

But I couldn't.

This wasn't just about business. It wasn't about legal loopholes and paperwork. This was about every person, like my parents and me, who had something stolen by Hayes and men like him. I had the chance to look the man in the eye and make damn sure he knew I wasn't just going to roll over and let him take what was mine.

Before I could second-guess myself, I grabbed my keys.

***

I white-knuckled the steering wheel as I pulled up to Bayside Ventures, my heartbeat drowning out every other thought. The corporate monstrosity towered over me - all glass, steel, and sharp edges, as dead inside as the drones who called it their nine-to-five prison. The kind of place that had nothing to do with Anchor Bay and everything to do with men like Hayes sinking their claws into small towns and turning them into playgrounds for the rich.

I reached for the door handle, but something made me pause. A flicker of movement out of the corner of my eye.

A car, idling half a block away.

I squinted through the fading light, a frown pulling at my brow. The second I saw who was behind the wheel, my stomach clenched.

Brooke.

She was tucked low in the driver's seat, a pair of binoculars pressed to her eyes as she watched the building. Streetlights cast sharp shadows over her face, highlighting the tight set of her jaw. She was focused, locked in, already way ahead of me.

Of course, she was.

Guilt twisted in my gut. She'd told me to stay out of it. She was trying to handle this by the book, and here I was, ready to charge in like an idiot. But I couldn't just leave or shake the thought of her sitting here alone, staking out a man like Hayes without backup.

I moved toward her car, sticking to the shadows, keeping my steps light. When I reached her window, I tapped on it lightly.

Brooke jumped like I'd fired a gun. Her head whipped around, eyes wide with shock that immediately narrowed into something much sharper—anger.

Yeah. I was in trouble.

Chapter Five

BROOKE

I clenched my jaw, my grip tightening on the steering wheel as I rolled down the window. "What the hell are you doing here?" I hissed, keeping my voice low.

Theo held up his hands, all fake innocence. "I found a connection between Hayes and a company buying up local businesses. Thought I'd check it out myself."

I exhaled sharply. "I told you to let me handle this."

"And I told you I couldn't sit this one out," he shot back, his voice calm but firm. His gaze flicked toward the building before coming back to me. "Look, we're both here now. Two sets of eyes are better than one, right?"

I closed my eyes briefly, forcing myself to breathe through the frustration. "Hayes might be meeting someone here tonight," I admitted, keeping my voice measured. "Got a tip. No way I was letting that slip through my fingers."

Theo nodded, looking half-impressed, half-annoyed. "Would it have killed you to call me?"

I fixed him with a hard stare. "Stay out of this, Theo," I said, the words coming out sharper than I intended. "I'm trying to protect you."

He opened his mouth—probably to argue—but my focus snapped to the movement at the building's entrance. "Theo," I whispered, tilting my head toward the glass doors.

We both turned, eyes locking on Rick Hayes as he exited the building. He still carried himself with that same smug, bulldog-like arrogance, shoulders hunched forward like he dared the world to challenge him. But there was something else tonight—something twitchy in how he glanced over his shoulder before hurrying toward the parking garage.

"Shit," I muttered, already fumbling with my seatbelt. "He's on the move."

My fingers flew to the door handle, my pulse hammering as I opened the door. The cold night air bit at my skin, but I barely noticed. My attention was locked on Hayes as he disappeared into the shadows of the parking garage.

Theo followed, his steps falling in sync with mine. I wanted to send him back and tell him to let me do my job, but there wasn't time for that now.

The parking garage rose before us like a concrete fortress, its shadows deep and corners menacing, reeking of car fumes and grease. We could hear Hayes above, his frantic steps ringing off the concrete as he raced upward. I crouched low, slipping between parked vehicles, moving across the grimy concrete without a sound. The flickering overhead fluorescents made everything feel distorted, throwing broken shadows across the rows of empty cars.

Third level.

I spotted Hayes rounding a corner up ahead. My heart pounded as I picked up the pace. The lights above continued their erratic flickering, sending shifting patterns across the garage.

A voice shattered the silence.

"I know you're following me."

I froze, pressing myself against a concrete pillar. I threw a hand up, silently motioning Theo to do the same. He obeyed—barely—I could see the tension coiled in his body, his fists clenched at his sides.

Hayes' voice echoed, bouncing off the empty space. "Playing detective, are we? Sticking your nose in business that'll get it cut off?"

My fingers brushed over my holster as I exchanged a look with Theo. Stay back, I warned him with my eyes.

"Why don't you come out and face me?" Hayes taunted, his voice slithering through the shadows. "Or are you too much of a coward?"

My grip tightened around my holster. Hayes knew someone was following him, but he didn't know who. That was my advantage. If I played this right, I could—

Before I could react, Theo barreled past me.

"Dammit," I hissed, reaching for him, but my fingers only skimmed the fabric of his sleeve before he tore away, striding straight into the open.

"I'm right here, you piece of shit," Theo growled, stepping out from behind an SUV.

Hayes whirled around, surprise flickering in his beady eyes before twisting into amusement. "Well, if it isn't Theo Morgan," he drawled. "Like a counterfeit coin, you keep showing up where you're not wanted."

My heart pounded as I pressed forward, keeping to the shadows between the parked cars, my fingers steady on my weapon. Theo was acting on emotion, and Hayes was dangerous. If this went sideways, I needed to be close enough to stop it.

"Game over, Hayes," Theo said, his voice low and steady, but I could hear the restrained fury beneath it. "I've got you figured out—strong-arming local businesses, pushing them to sell. Real classy operation you've got."

Hayes laughed, the sound scraping against the parking garage walls like steel on concrete. "You don't know anything, boy. You're in way over your head."

Theo took another step forward. "I know enough. You destroyed my family's bar years ago. Now you're back, doing the same thing to other hardworking people. But it ends now."

Hayes' eyes darkened, his smirk faltering momentarily before he recovered. "You should've learned your lesson the first time, Morgan. Some things are bigger than your pathetic little bar."

I clenched my jaw, frustration bubbling up inside me. Theo was walking straight into Hayes' trap—letting himself get provoked, giving Hayes the distraction he wanted. I needed to shut this down before it got worse.

"That's enough," I snapped, stepping into view, my badge held high. "Rick Hayes, you're coming with me."

Hayes' entire body went rigid, his eyes darting between me and Theo. He looked cornered, like a rat in a maze. Then, just as quickly, his expression morphed into a sneer.

"You've got nothing on me," he spat. "This is harassment."

I took a measured step closer, keeping my voice even. "We have evidence linking you to the vandalism of local businesses. Come quietly, and we can sort this out at the station."

Hayes scoffed, his smirk turning razor-sharp. "Evidence? I doubt that very much. You've got nothing but suspicions and the ramblings of a washed-up bartender."

I saw the shift in Theo a split second before it happened—the way his shoulders bunched and his fists clenched at his sides.

"Theo, don't—"

Too late.

Theo lunged.

His fist slammed into Hayes' jaw with a sickening crack, echoing through the parking garage. Hayes staggered back, his expression twisting into fury.

"Shit," I swore, already moving.

Hayes recovered fast and charged, ramming his knee into Theo's gut. The two collided, fists flying, bodies slamming into a concrete support pillar as they threw wild punches.

"Both of you, knock it off! Now!" My voice rang out, bouncing off the walls.

They didn't listen.

Theo drove Hayes back against the pillar, forearm pressing into his windpipe. Hayes gasped, clawing at his arm, his face turning red.

I didn't think. I moved.

I shoved my shoulder between them, forcing Theo back with a hard push to his chest.

"Enough!" I barked, my pulse hammering.

Theo stumbled but didn't resist, his fists still clenched, rage simmering just beneath the surface. Hayes doubled over, coughing, his hands rubbing at his throat—but that damn smirk was already creeping back across his bloody lips.

I turned on Theo, my voice sharp. "What the hell are you doing? Do you want to get yourself arrested?"

His jaw was tight, chest heaving, but something flickered across his face—regret. He exhaled sharply but said nothing.

That flicker of hesitation was all Hayes needed.

A shift. A blur of motion.

Hayes moved. Fast.

Too fast.

I barely had time to process it—he twisted, his hand flying to his pocket as he shoved off the column.

The glint of metal caught the light. A switchblade.

I reached for my weapon, but before I could draw, Hayes lunged—not at Theo, but at me.

I saw it too late.

The blade arced toward me, sharp and unforgiving. Then, suddenly—Theo.

He moved before I could, shoving me back just as the knife sliced through the air.

The sickening sound of tearing fabric. A sharp inhale.

Theo gritted his teeth, stumbling, blood already blooming across his forearm.

Fury shot through me. I spun back toward Hayes, slamming him against the column, wrenching the blade from his grip.

But then Theo swayed.

Instinct overruled training—I turned, grabbing Theo's arm to steady him.

The moment my grip loosened, Hayes took his shot.

A sharp shove, a twist of his body—and he was free.

I whipped around just as he bolted. His footsteps pounded against the concrete, disappearing toward the stairwell before I could react.

Damn it.

I moved to chase, but Theo's weight shifted against me, and I cursed, torn between pursuing the bastard and making sure Theo wasn't about to hit the ground.

Theo let out a rough breath, jaw clenched. "Go," he gritted out. "I'll be fine."

But leaving him bleeding? Not a damn chance.

"Damn it!" I swore, my eyes flicking toward the stairwell. Hayes was gone.

My jaw clenched, frustration burning through me, but it was drowned out by something stronger—concern.

I turned back to Theo. Blood seeped through the tear in his sleeve, dripping down his arm. His jaw was tight, his expression unreadable, but his skin had gone a shade too pale.

I took a step closer, reaching for his arm. "Are you okay?"

"Peachy," he muttered, biting back a grimace as he tried—and failed—to stand up straight.

"Like hell you are," I snapped, reaching for my radio. "Dispatch, we need medical and backup at my location ASAP. Suspect is fleeing on foot, parking garage stairwell."

Theo shifted beside me, his breathing tight. "Brooke, go after him."

I ignored him, pressing my radio again. "I need a unit in pursuit—now."

The response crackled through my earpiece, but my focus stayed locked on Theo. His arm was still bleeding, his stance unsteady, his face paler than I liked.

"I'm fine," he said, reading the concern on my face.

"You're bleeding, Theo," I shot back. "So unless you suddenly got a degree in emergency medicine, shut up and let me handle this."

His lips twitched like he wanted to argue, but sirens cut through the night, and relief sagged my shoulders as flashing red-and-blue lights swept across the parking structure.

A white van rolled in behind the cruisers, and as the back doors swung open, I let out a slow breath at the sight of Lucas climbing out. The easy confidence in his step, the casual way he slung his bag over his shoulder—it didn't erase the chaos around us, but damn, it helped.

"Figures it'd be you two," Lucas called, amusement lacing his voice even as he took in the scene. "Alright, who's bleeding?"

I stepped aside, my hand still on Theo's uninjured arm, steadying him. "That would be Mr. 'I'm fine' over here."

Theo scoffed. "I've had worse."

Lucas arched a brow. "Yeah? Let's see it."

As Lucas went to work, I finally exhaled, my heartbeat still a little too fast, my body still too wired with adrenaline. I dragged my gaze away from Theo's bloodied sleeve, scanning the stairwell.

Hayes was gone.

For now.

Chapter Six

THEO

"What'd you get yourself into this time, Morgan?" Lucas teased, kneeling to check my arm.

I exhaled sharply, watching the blood soak into the gauze. "Made sure Brooke didn't take a knife to the gut."

Lucas's smirk faded. He glanced at Brooke, then back at me. "Hell."

"Yeah."

Lucas didn't say anything else as he worked, his movements quick and practiced.

The pain wasn't unbearable, but it was enough to remind me just how close that blade had come to Brooke.

Hayes got away. Brooke was quiet. Too quiet.

Lucas worked quickly, his hands steady as he wrapped my arm. He didn't say much—just the usual EMT reassurances—but his gaze kept flicking toward Brooke, who hovered nearby, gripping her radio like it was the only thing keeping her grounded.

"You riding with him?" Lucas asked, his voice quieter now.

I turned my head just in time to see Brooke's jaw tighten. "I can't."

She didn't even look at me when she said it.

Lucas frowned, but he didn't push. And honestly, neither did I.

Because I already knew the truth.

She was pulling away.

The ambulance doors shut, and as the rig pulled away, I watched Brooke grow smaller and smaller through the back window, standing alone in the parking lot like she was trying to convince herself she'd done the right thing.

Maybe she had.

***

The Rusty Anchor was a ghost of itself today. I let out a long breath, dragged my hand down my face, and forced myself up from the chair. My untouched water glass left a dark ring on the desk's weathered surface, beads of moisture tracking down its sides. The bandage around my arm felt tight, each throb underneath a stark reminder of last night's mess.

Lucas had done his job—patched me up, hauled me to the hospital, made sure I didn't shrug off getting stitches. But it wasn't his voice I wanted to hear.

It was Brooke's.

But she hadn't come to the hospital. Hadn't called. Hadn't even checked in.

I sighed, pushing open my office door and stepping into the empty bar. The usual hum of conversation, clinking glasses, and music was missing, replaced by silence and the faint creak of the floorboards under my boots.

"Guess it's just you and me again," I muttered to the bar, my voice rough.

A quiet chuckle from the doorway made me look up.

Lucas.

He leaned against the frame, his EMT bag slung over one shoulder, looking too amused for my liking.

"Talking to furniture now?" he asked. "That bad, huh?"

I let out a huff of laughter, shaking my head. "What do you want, Lucas?"

"Just checking in," he said, stepping inside like he owned the place. "And, seeing if you've figured out that you're in love with Brooke yet."

My jaw tightened, but Lucas just smirked.

"Relax," he said, tossing his bag onto a stool. "I'm not here to meddle. Just saying you two have been orbiting each other for years. Maybe it's time to stop circling and just... land."

I exhaled, running a hand over my jaw. "She pulled away. Maybe that's my answer."

"Or," Lucas countered, leaning on the bar, "maybe she's scared. And maybe you need to remind her why it's worth it."

I didn't answer, but the words settled deep, sinking into the places I didn't want to examine.

Lucas clapped me on the shoulder and headed for the door, his voice easy as ever. "Think about it, man."

I sat there long after he left, my mind turning over every moment from the past few days. Every look, every hesitation, every time Brooke had chosen to run instead of face what was between us.

Lucas was right.

We'd been dancing around this for years, but now, when it finally came to a head, she was backing away.

I couldn't let that happen.

Not without a fight.

With renewed determination, I grabbed my keys and headed for the door.

I knew where she'd be.

The same place she always went when she needed to think.

BROOKE

I stared at my reflection in the dim light of my bathroom, taking in the dark circles beneath my eyes and the exhaustion carved into my features. Another night without sleep, another day refusing to give me a break. My mind kept looping the same images—the glint of the knife, the sharp bloom of red on Theo's sleeve, the look in his eyes that wasn't just pain.

I turned on the faucet and splashed cold water onto my face, the shock helping to ground me, if only for a second. As I reached for a towel, my gaze landed on my phone, sitting silently on the counter. No messages. No missed calls.

Theo hadn't reached out.

I knew what I needed to do. Pick up the phone, call Theo, and apologize for running away when I should have been there. But every time my fingers hovered over his name, doubt crawled in.

Would he blame me for what happened? Was this the moment he finally realized I was more trouble than I was worth?

I exhaled sharply and dropped the phone, pressing my fingers to my temples as if I could rub away the mess in my head.

I needed to get out.

Keys in hand, I left my apartment, letting muscle memory guide me as I drove. I wasn't sure where I was heading, but my hands knew before my mind did. When the old lighthouse loomed in the distance, standing tall against the storm-heavy sky, I realized I'd known all along.

The wind was sharp as I stepped out of the car, the briny scent of the sea filling my lungs. Gravel crunched beneath my boots as I made my way up the worn path, the lighthouse standing like an old friend welcoming me back. I'd been coming here for years, ever since I was a kid—the one place that always felt separate from everything else, where the world couldn't reach me.

I climbed the steps and gripped the railing at the top, staring at the dark water below. The waves crashed against the rocks in a rhythm that should have been calming, but my mind wouldn't settle.

I wasn't supposed to be here.

I was supposed to be at the Rusty Anchor, checking on Theo, ensuring he was okay. But instead, I was here, falling into old habits—running when things got too hard, too real.

"Still running to your favorite hideout, I see."

The voice behind me sent a jolt through my chest.

I turned sharply, my pulse kicking up. Theo stood there, wind ruffling his dark hair, his bandaged arm tucked close to his side. His eyes were unreadable, but something in them pinned me in place.

He stepped forward, his voice quieter this time. "You weren't at the hospital."

I swallowed hard. "I couldn't be."

"Why not?" Another step closer. "I needed you, Brooke."

His words knocked the air from my lungs. My fingers curled around the railing, tight enough that my knuckles blanched white and the cold metal dug under my nails. "I'm sorry," I managed, my voice barely carrying over the wind. "I couldn't... I couldn't face you. Not after everything."

Theo's stern facade wavered, but his stance remained firm. "What are you talking about? None of this is on you."

I squeezed my eyes shut against the burning behind them. "I should have protected you. Stopped you from going after Hayes."

"That was my choice," Theo said, his voice firm but gentle. "Not yours."

His hand found my arm, his touch warm despite the bite in the air. My eyes snapped open, locking onto his.

"What are you *really* afraid of, Brooke?" he asked, his voice low, steady. "That I got hurt? Or that you care too much?"

The words cut straight through me.

I turned away, gripping the railing like it was the only thing keeping me upright. Below, the waves crashed violently against the rocks, mirroring the storm churning inside me.

"Both," I whispered.

I bit down on my lower lip, the weight of my admission settling in. There was no taking it back now. No pretending I hadn't said it.

"I care about you, Theo." The words felt fragile, too raw. "More than I should. And that scares the hell out of me."

Theo stepped closer, his presence solid, grounding. His palm found the small of my back, his warmth seeping through the fabric of my jacket.

"Why does it scare you?" he asked, his voice barely above a whisper.

I closed my eyes, swallowing past the knot tightening in my throat. "Because caring means you can get hurt. It means you have something to lose."

"Or something to gain," Theo countered.

His fingers brushed my arm, slow and careful, before he turned me to face him. My pulse thundered as his hazel eyes locked onto mine, steady and sure.

"Brooke, I've been in love with you for years," he said, the words filled with quiet certainty. "Honestly, I thought you knew."

I stared at him, my breath hitching, my mind struggling to catch up. "You... you love me?" The words barely made it past my lips.

Theo let out a small, almost self-conscious chuckle. "Yeah, well. I've never been great at hiding things."

His confession sent a new wave of panic and longing crashing into me. I held his gaze, my heart pounding so hard it felt impossible to speak. I wanted to say something, anything, but the words stuck, tangled with the emotions I hadn't let myself feel until now.

Theo's hand came up, his fingers warm and steady as they cupped my cheek. His thumb brushed softly over my skin, the touch so gentle it made my chest ache.

"I know you're scared," he murmured, his voice low, steady. "But I'm scared too—scared of never knowing what this could be if we don't take the chance."

I leaned into his touch, my eyes fluttering closed for a moment. When I opened them again, he was even closer, his breath warm against my skin, his presence wrapping around me.

"I can't lose you," I whispered, my voice barely holding steady. "Not you, Theo. I need you."

His hand tightened ever so slightly, anchoring me. "You won't," he promised, his voice like a quiet vow. "I'm not going anywhere. I never have."

I pressed into his palm, my eyes falling shut again. The wind howled around us, pulling at my hair and my jacket, but I didn't feel any of it. All I felt was Theo—solid, warm, mine.

The words slipped out before I could stop them. "I love you too."

Chapter Seven

♥

THEO

My heart stuttered at Brooke's words. I thought I'd imagined them for a moment—that the howling wind had twisted her voice into what I desperately wanted to hear. But when I looked into her eyes and saw vulnerability mixed with something fierce and sure, I knew.

She meant it.

"Say it again," I murmured, needing to hear the words once more.

Brooke's lips curved into a soft smile, her eyes never leaving mine. "I love you, Theo."

That was all it took.

I closed the distance between us, pressing my lips to hers. She melted into me instantly, her arms wrapping around my neck as she kissed me back with a passion that made my head spin.

Her lips were soft against mine, tasting faintly of mint and something uniquely her. I pulled her closer, my good arm wrapping around her waist as I deepened the kiss.

Brooke let out a soft moan that sent electricity through my body. She wove her fingers through my hair, pulling me closer as she pressed against me. The wind gusted around us, but I couldn't focus on anything except how warm she felt, how perfectly she melded into me, like two pieces of a puzzle finally clicking into place.

When we finally broke apart, breathless, I rested my forehead against hers. Brooke's eyes fluttered open, dark with desire, a flush spreading across her cheeks.

"Wow," she whispered, her voice thick with desire. "We should have done that a long time ago."

I grinned, pulling her closer. "Better late than never."

Brooke smiled back, her eyes sparkling with love and desire. She leaned in and kissed me again, slower this time but no less passionate. Her fingers traced along my jaw as she deepened the kiss, drawing a low groan from my throat.

I gently backed her against the lighthouse wall, never breaking the kiss. The rough stone pressed against her back as I trailed my lips down her neck, savoring the soft gasp that escaped her. My hands roamed over her curves, memorizing every dip and swell.

"Theo," she breathed, her voice thick with want. "I want you."

I met her intense stare as I lowered myself to my knees before her. Brooke's breath caught, understanding dawning in her widening eyes. Never breaking our connection, I slowly lifted her shirt. Her muscles tensed in anticipation, and her breath caught as I slowly unbuttoned her jeans, sliding them down her legs along with her underwear. The cool air hit her heated skin, raising goosebumps. I pressed soft kisses along her thighs, savoring her quiet gasps.

My hands gripped her hips, steadying her as I leaned in and inhaled Brooke's intoxicating scent deeply. The tangy sweetness of her arousal filled my senses, igniting a primal hunger within me.

Brooke's breath hitched as I gently parted her thighs. I took my time, trailing kisses along sensitive skin, building her anticipation.

When I finally tasted her, Brooke's essence exploded across my tongue, an intoxicating blend of honey and musk that made my head spin. I savor that first taste, committing every nuance to memory. My tongue explores her folds deliberately, tracing each dip and curve. She was silky smooth against my lips, warm and inviting.

Brooke moaned low in her throat, her fingers tangled in my hair, urging me closer. I took my time, exploring every inch of her with slow, deliberate strokes.

Brooke's legs trembled as I circled her clit. Her head fell against the lighthouse wall, eyes fluttering closed in pleasure. I glanced up, taking in the sight of her - flushed cheeks, parted lips, wholly lost in sensation.

I increased my pace, circling her clit as I slid two fingers inside her. Brooke gasped, her hips rocking against my mouth.

"God, Brooke," I murmured against her heated skin. "You taste incredible. Like honey and the sea."

She whimpered in response, her hips bucking more insistently against my mouth. I redoubled my efforts, circling her clit with firm strokes of my tongue as I curled my fingers inside her. Brooke's thighs trembled on either side of my head, her fingers tightening in my hair as she got closer to the edge.

"Oh god, Theo," she moaned, her voice breathless and needy.

I looked up, watching her face as I pleasured her. Brooke's eyes were squeezed shut, her bottom lip caught between her teeth as she tried to muffle her sounds of pleasure. The sight of her coming undone because of me was intoxicating.

"Let go, Brooke," I murmured against her heated skin. "I want to hear you."

"Theo," she whimpered, her nails digging into the rough stone of the lighthouse wall. "Oh god, I'm... I'm... "

I didn't give her a chance to finish as I drove her over the edge with a deep, lingering kiss against her clit, my fingers pumping in and out of her hot, tight body.

Brooke's eyes flew open, their intensity taking my breath away. She cried out, her orgasm ripping through her body, and I didn't stop until she'd ridden out every last wave of pleasure.

Brooke slumped against the lighthouse wall, breathless, her chest rising and falling rapidly. Looking into her eyes, blazing with want, made my pulse race.

"Come here," she whispered, fingers curling into my shirt to pull me closer.

Rising to meet her, I pressed my body against hers, desire coursing through me. She was still shaking, her skin hot under my touch. I held her face between my palms, taking in every detail - her messed hair, her lips red and full, her eyes heavy with need.

"You're so damn beautiful," I whispered, running my thumb across her bottom lip.

Her tongue flicked out, tasting herself, and the sensation shot straight through me. I pressed my forehead to hers, groaning softly as I tried to maintain control.

"Brooke," I breathed, my voice rough with want. "I can't wait, I have to be inside you. To feel you wrapped around me, hot and tight."

She whimpered softly, her hips rocking against mine.

Brooke's hands slid down my chest, her fingers deftly unfastening my jeans. I groaned as she pushed them down, freeing my aching erection. Her hand wrapped around me, stroking slowly.

With trembling hands, I reached down into my pocket and pulled out a small foil packet. My fingers fumbled slightly as I tore it open, the anticipation making my movements clumsy. Brooke's eyes were locked on mine, dark with desire, as I rolled the condom on.

The thin latex felt cool against my heated skin. I took a deep breath, steadying myself. This felt monumental—years of longing and unspoken feelings culminating in this moment. I wanted to savor every second.

Brooke's fingers traced along my length, her touch feather-light and teasing. A shiver ran through me at the contact. She guided me to her entrance, both of us trembling with need.

"I want you inside me," she whispered, her voice husky with desire. "Now."

I didn't need to be told twice. I lifted her, pinning her against the lighthouse wall as she wrapped her legs around my waist. With one smooth thrust, I buried myself inside her tight, wet heat.

We both cried out at the sensation. Brooke's nails dug into my shoulders as she adjusted to my size. I held still, savoring the feeling of finally being joined with her like this.

"You feel incredible," I murmured against her neck, pressing soft kisses to her heated skin.

"Theo," Brooke gasped, her legs tightening around my waist. "Please... move."

Brooke gasped as I slowly withdrew before thrusting back in, setting a steady rhythm that had us both moaning. Brooke's head fell back against the lighthouse wall, her eyes fluttering closed in pleasure as I drove into her again and again.

The wind whipped around us, carrying the sound of crashing waves, but I barely noticed. All I could focus on was Brooke—the way she felt wrapped around me, hot and tight, the little gasps and moans that escaped her with each thrust, and the way her fingers dug into my shoulders.

I trailed kisses along her neck, savoring the salty-sweet taste of her skin. "God, Brooke," I groaned against her throat. "So fucking perfect."

Brooke moaned in response, her hips rocking to meet my thrusts. Her legs tightened around my waist, drawing me in deeper. I could feel her trembling against me, her inner walls fluttering around my length as she got closer to the edge.

"Theo," she gasped, her voice breathy and desperate. "I'm so close. Please... harder."

I groaned at her words, my pace growing frantic as I drove into Brooke again and again. Her body was molten heat around me, drawing me deeper with each thrust. I shifted my angle slightly, hitting a spot deep inside her that made her cry out in pleasure.

"Yes," Brooke whimpered, her nails raking down my back. "Right there. Don't stop."

I drove into her harder, faster, chasing both our releases. I kept my angle, hitting that spot repeatedly as I felt Brooke tightening around me. Her breath came in short pants, her body trembling as she approached the edge.

"Come for me, Brooke," I urged, my voice rough with desire. "Let go. I want to feel you come around me."

A keening cry escaped her lips as she shattered. Her back arched, pressing her breasts against my chest as waves of pleasure wracked her body. The feeling of her pulsing around me, hot and tight, was my undoing.

With a guttural groan, I buried myself deep inside her as my own orgasm crashed over me. Wave after wave of intense pleasure coursed through my body as I came hard inside her.

We clung to each other, still joined together, panting and spent, for several long moments, both trembling in the aftermath. Finally, I slid out of her and lowered her to the floor of the lighthouse.

Brooke leaned against me, and I wrapped my arms around her, holding her close as our heartbeats slowly returned to normal.

Brooke's fingers traced along my jaw, her touch feather-light. Her blue eyes sparkled with love and lingering desire as she gazed at me. A soft smile played at her lips, slightly swollen from our passionate kisses.

"Damn," she murmured, her voice still husky. "All these years wasted when we could've been doing that?"

A soft laugh escaped me as I drew her closer, her warmth against me making my head spin in the best way. "Better late than never," I said again, smiling at my repetition.

Brooke hummed in response, nestling her head against my chest. Everything else fell away momentarily as we stood wrapped in each other, the coastal wind whipping around us. The old lighthouse groaned, the sound yanking me back to the present.

I let out a satisfied sigh, stretching before turning my head to look at Brooke. "As much as I'd love to stay here all night, we should probably get dressed before we traumatize some unsuspecting fisherman."

Brooke groaned, running a hand over her face. "Yeah, pretty sure a cop getting busted for indecent exposure would be hard to live down."

I chuckled softly as we reluctantly untangled ourselves and gathered our scattered clothing. The cool air raised goosebumps on my skin, but I couldn't stop smiling as I watched Brooke shimmy back into her jeans.

Fully dressed now, I drew her in close, caught by an irresistible urge to kiss her again. Brooke sank against me, pulling herself closer as her arms found their way around my neck, turning my gentle kiss into something heated. When we parted, I caught the glint in her eyes.

"So," she whispered, twirling my hair between her fingers. "What happens now?"

I brushed my thumb over her cheek, my other hand resting on her back. "That depends," I said, my voice low but sure. "Are you asking as my best friend or as the woman I just made love to in an abandoned lighthouse?"

Brooke huffed a quiet laugh, but I didn't miss the flicker of something in her expression. "Both."

I exhaled, my forehead dipping to rest lightly against hers. "Well, I guess the answer is the same either way." I tilted her chin up, meeting her gaze. "I want this. You. Us."

Her fingers tensed slightly where they rested against my shoulders. "You sure?" she asked softly, her usual confidence giving way to something vulnerable. "We've been friends for a long time, Theo. There's no going back after this."

I cupped her face, my thumb sweeping over her bottom lip. "Brooke, I don't want to go back." The words came easily because they were the truth. "I think part of me has always wanted this. I just..." I exhaled sharply, shaking my head with a quiet chuckle. "Hell, I think I was scared of screwing it up."

Brooke studied me for a long moment, then smirked, a familiar teasing glint in her eyes. "Well, if tonight's anything to go by, I'd say we're doing just fine."

I groaned, my head dropping to her shoulder as she laughed. "I was trying to be serious for once, Taylor."

"I know," she murmured, her fingers threading through my hair. Then, more softly, "I want this too."

I pulled back just enough to look at her, my chest tightening at the sight of her flushed, smiling, looking at me like maybe she'd been waiting for this just as long as I had. "Then that settles it."

Her lips twitched. "Oh? Just like that?"

I shrugged, giving her a lopsided grin. "Just like that. We take it one day at a time. No overthinking, no second-guessing. Just us."

Brooke exhaled, then nodded, something settling in her expression. "Yeah. Okay."

I grinned and tugged her in for another kiss, slow and lingering. "Good. But just so we're clear, I fully intend to make up for all those wasted years."

Brooke smirked against my lips. "Yeah? We'll see if you can keep up, Morgan."

I chuckled, tucking her against my side as we started back down the lighthouse steps, the moment between us lighter now.

No going back. And for the first time, I didn't want to.

Epilogue

♥

BROOKE

The Rusty Anchor pulsed with life, the newly installed lights casting a warm glow over the sidewalk. Inside, the grand reopening buzzed with energy—ice clinking in glasses, bursts of laughter breaking through the hum of conversation, the familiar mix of salt air and weathered timber settling into something that felt like home.

I propped myself against the bar, watching Theo move behind the counter like he owned the room. Which, of course, he did.

He worked effortlessly—mixing drinks, tossing out one-liners, flashing that signature grin that made everyone feel like a regular. I'd seen him like this a thousand times before, but tonight felt different. Because, for the first time, I let myself admit how much I loved seeing him like this.

How much I loved him.

"You gonna stand there all night, or you actually ordering?"

Theo's voice pulled me back, his hazel eyes twinkling with amusement.

I smirked. "I think I'll let you surprise me."

He leaned in, voice dropping just for me. "Careful, Officer Taylor. I've been known to get creative."

Before I could respond, Olivia and Jack appeared, arms wrapped around each other.

"This place looks amazing," Olivia said, spinning to take in the transformation. "Seriously, Theo, I'm impressed."

Theo shrugged, flicking a glance my way. "Can't take all the credit—had some help."

Jack's smirk was instant, his gaze bouncing between us. "Oh, is that what you two are calling it now?"

I shot him a warning look. "Watch it, Lawson. I'm still a cop."

Jack held up his hands in surrender, grinning. "Noted."

As Olivia dragged him off to mingle, I turned back to Theo.

The bar noise faded, the crowd disappearing into the background. His expression softened, something deeper settling in his eyes.

"This place doesn't feel complete without you here," he said, his voice quieter now.

I raised an eyebrow. "Smooth, Morgan."

His lips twitched, but his gaze didn't waver. "Not just tonight. Every day. You're part of this now—part of me."

My breath caught. For years, I would've scoffed at words like that. But now? Now, all I felt was warmth.

I let a slow smile form. "You're getting pretty good at this sweet-talking thing."

"Good." Theo stepped closer, his voice more certain. "Because I'm not stopping."

And then his lips were on mine.

The bar exploded with hoots and whistles, but they faded to background noise as I grabbed his shirt, yanking him closer and deepening the kiss.

When we finally came up for air, I rested my forehead against his, chuckling at all the grinning faces turned our way. "Well, there goes our attempt at subtlety."

Theo's hands stayed steady on my waist as he smirked. "Let them stare. I've got nothing to hide."

As the music picked up and the crowd swayed around us, I leaned into him, letting the moment settle, letting myself sink into it.

It had taken us years to get here.

But looking at Theo now, I knew—some things were worth the wait.

***

Dear Reader,

Thank you so much for reading *Love's Anchor*! I hope you adored Theo and Brooke's journey from friendship to something so much more. Their story was filled with banter, tension, and plenty of heart, and I'm beyond grateful you came along for the ride.

If you enjoyed the book, I'd love it if you took a moment to leave a review. Reviews help authors like me connect with more readers, and even just a few words make a world of difference!

Your support means everything, and I can't wait to bring you more love stories soon!

With gratitude,

Hana York

***

Ready for More?

If you loved *Love's Anchor*, you won't want to miss what's coming next! *On Call for You* is a sizzling, small-town forbidden love romance featuring Lucas Carter—a dedicated EMT who knows better than to mix work with romance... until he meets the fiery new doctor in town.

Sophie Whitaker is smart, driven, and impossible to ignore. From the moment they meet, Lucas feels the pull—only to realize, too late, that she's his best friend's little sister.

Sophie Whitaker has spent years proving herself in the medical field, determined to be seen for her skills—not underestimated because of her size. The last thing she needs is to fall for a man who makes her lose focus—especially when that man is her brother's best friend.

Fate throws them together, and their undeniable attraction becomes impossible to ignore. But breaking the rules has consequences... and loving each other might be the biggest risk of all.

Keep reading for a sneak peek at Chapter One of *On Call for You* – Available on Amazon on March 4th, 2025!

Sneak Peak of On Call for You

♥

LUCAS

The emergency room pulsed with my favorite kind of mayhem. My heart raced as I maneuvered the stretcher through the sliding doors while my partner's voice cut through the din.

"Male, mid-fifties, went down at the marina!"

Sharp hospital disinfectant stung my nostrils, mixing with the controlled chaos of voices as staff parted the way ahead. I kept one hand steady on the stretcher, the other on the patient's arm—a silent reassurance, even as my mind raced through the vitals, we'd barely managed to stabilize en route.

"BP was 68 over 40," I called out, my voice cutting through the noise. "Pulse is weak but steady now. Couldn't get a clear history before he went out."

"Room three is open," a nurse directed, motioning toward the far end of the ER.

I nodded and moved quickly, my boots squeaking against the linoleum. Just as I reached the exam bay, a petite redhead in scrubs stepped into my path, clipboard in hand and copper curls pinned back beneath a surgical cap.

"Vitals?" she asked, her tone crisp, her gaze flicking from me to the patient.

I blinked. I'd worked with nearly every doctor at Anchor Bay General but didn't recognize her. New. That much was obvious. But the way she took control—calm, efficient like she'd been running this ER for years—caught me off guard.

"BP's holding steady at 92 over 62 now," I said, watching as she leaned over the stretcher, her hands methodical as she assessed the patient. "Pulse is regular but weak. Possible cardiac history, but no confirmation yet."

"Good work stabilizing him." She flashed me a quick, professional smile—businesslike but oddly disarming.

Before I could process why she seemed vaguely familiar, she was already issuing orders. "Push fluids and start a second line," she said to a nurse before turning back to me. "Did he mention any meds or allergies before he lost consciousness?"

"No," I said, shaking my head. "We didn't get that far before he crashed."

Her lips pressed into a thin line as she focused on the patient, her movements efficient as she checked his airway. "Thanks for getting him here in one piece, Carter," she said absently, like she'd memorized my name from my badge.

"Anytime, Doc," I replied, though something about her gave me pause.

She hesitated for a fraction of a second, her green eyes flicking up to meet mine. "Sophie," she corrected, her voice professional but not unfriendly. "Just started here last week."

A flicker of something I couldn't quite name settled in my chest.

Sophie.

Recognition tugged at me, but I couldn't place it.

"Lucas," I offered, my gaze lingering on her longer than it should have.

"Nice to meet you, Lucas," she said, turning back to the patient.

I stepped aside, my job done, but my mind wasn't ready to let it go. She was more than competent, but there was something else. A quiet intensity. And just the faintest hint of a chip on her shoulder, like she was ready to prove something.

It shouldn't have mattered. I worked with new doctors all the time.

So why the hell couldn't I shake the feeling that I'd seen her somewhere before?

***

I wound up at The Rusty Anchor that evening, hunched over a drink I'd definitely earned after the day I'd had. The usual bar noise swirled around me—people talking, some twangy country song playing somewhere—but it was all just white noise at that point. My mind was somewhere else.

Or rather, on someone else.

Sophie.

The sharp-eyed redhead from the ER had been stuck in my head all day, and I couldn't decide if it was her confidence, quick hands, or how she'd looked at me like she was trying to figure out a puzzle—and I was the missing piece.

I took another sip of my drink, willing the thought away when a familiar voice cut through the noise.

"Lucas!"

I turned just as Nate Whitaker—Detective, best friend, and all-around pain in my ass—grinned his way through the crowded bar and clapped a hand on my shoulder.

"Damn, man, you look like you've been through it today," he said, nodding toward my drink.

"Long shift." I took another sip, not about to mention the part where I couldn't stop thinking about a certain ER doc.

"Well, I got someone you gotta meet," Nate continued, motioning behind him. "My little sister, Sophie. She finally moved back after being away forever."

The glass froze halfway to my lips.

No. Freaking. Way.

I set my drink down very carefully because otherwise, I might drop it.

Sophie.

The redhead from the ER. The woman I'd spent all day trying to forget.

I knew Nate had a sister, but I'd never met her. He'd mentioned her over the years—how she was off at some fancy medical school, how she worked in a big-city hospital, how she was too damn stubborn for her own good. But none of that had prepared me for the woman standing in front of me now.

Sophie's green eyes widened slightly in recognition, but instead of looking shocked, she looked amused. Like she'd already put this together and was just waiting to see how long it would take me to catch up.

"You've got to be kidding me," I muttered, raking a hand through my hair as the pieces clicked into place.

Her lips twitched in that same confident, teasing way I'd seen earlier. "Small world," she said lightly.

"Too small," I muttered.

Nate's brow furrowed as he glanced between us. "Wait a minute. You two know each other?"

Sophie cocked her head nonchalantly. "Oh, we've met. Lucas was the EMT on my first trauma case at Anchor Bay General."

I shifted my weight, keeping my voice steady despite the sudden heat crawling up my neck. "All part of the job."

Nate laughed, completely missing how Sophie and I were still staring at each other. "Look at that—saving me the introductions after all."

Yeah. Saving. That was one way to put it.

I flicked my gaze back to Sophie, who looked entirely too pleased with this little twist of fate.

Gorgeous, sharp-witted, and completely off-limits.

Fantastic.

She leaned in slightly, her voice just low enough for only me to hear. "Looks like we'll be seeing a lot more of each other, Lucas."

Her perfume—something light and floral, something that shouldn't make my brain short-circuit but absolutely did—wrapped around me. I swallowed hard, acutely aware of how close she was, how easy it would be to turn my head and...

Nope. Bad idea.

"I guess so," I managed, my voice rougher than I meant for it to be.

Before I could get my bearings, Nate clapped a hand on my back, utterly oblivious to the fact that I was currently having a mild crisis over his sister.

"Hey, I have an idea. Why don't you go with Sophie to the presentation she's doing tomorrow?" he suggested. "I've got a case to work, but I don't want her going alone and getting lost."

I opened my mouth to shut that down—because spending more time with Sophie was very clearly a dangerous idea—but she beat me to it.

"That's not necessary," she said quickly. "I'm sure Lucas has better things to do with his time."

Probably. Definitely.

But then, for some reason, my mouth moved before my brain caught up.

"No, it's fine. I'd be happy to go with you."

Sophie's eyebrows lifted slightly as if she hadn't expected that answer. Hell, neither did I.

Her expression smoothed just as quickly, her voice carefully neutral. "Well, if you're sure. It's at one of the elementary schools on the outskirts of town."

I shifted my weight, fighting the ridiculous mix of nerves and anticipation curling in my gut. "I know exactly where that is. How's 8:30 tomorrow morning sound?"

Then she smiled. Not just any smile—one that hit me like a gut punch, slow and knowing like she already had me figured out.

"Perfect," she said, reaching for her phone. "I'll text you my address."

Great. Just great.

Tomorrow, I'd be spending the day alone with Sophie Whitaker.

I'd been in plenty of high-risk situations before, but being alone with Nate's little sister? That was a whole different kind of danger.

***On Call for You* hits Amazon on March 4, 2025!!**

Hana York Books

♥

Hearts on Desire Series

Sparks of Temptation

Love's Anchor

For a full list of titles, please visit Hana York's website

www.HanaYork.com

About the Author

Hana York writes fast-paced, heart-pounding contemporary romance packed with irresistible heroes, strong heroines, laugh-out-loud banter, and just the right amount of spice to keep things sizzling. Her books are for readers who love grumpy men falling hard, fierce women who don't need saving, and the kind of chemistry that sparks off the page.

When she's not crafting stories full of love, tension, and toe-curling moments, you'll find her daydreaming about small-town charm, plotting ridiculous meet-cutes, and consuming an unhealthy amount of coffee. She believes in happily-ever-afters, overprotective heroes who don't stand a chance against their heroines, and that every great love story should come with a side of sass.

If you love forced proximity, off-limits attraction, sizzling tension, and romance that makes your heart race, welcome to the world of Hana York!

Follow Hana York for new releases, exclusive content, and behind-the-scenes fun! Visit www.HanaYork.com for more!